MR. LAZY

by Roger Hargreaves

EGMONT

Mr Lazy lives in Sleepyland, which is a very lazy-looking and sleepy-like place.

The birds in Sleepyland fly so slowly they sometimes fall out of the sky.

The grass takes so long to grow it only needs cutting once a year.

Even the trees are lazy-looking and sleepy-like.

And do you know what time everybody gets up in Sleepyland?

The answer is, they don't get up in the morning.

They get up in the afternoon!

And, incidentally, this is what a Sleepyland clock looks like.

Everything takes so long to do there's only time for four hours a day!

Anyway, this story starts with Mr Lazy being fast asleep in bed. In Sleepyland they call that being slow asleep!

He spends rather a lot of time in bed. It's his favourite place to be!

He opened his eyes, yawned, yawned again – and went back to sleep.

Later, Mr Lazy opened his eyes again, yawned, yawned again, and went back to sleep again.

Much later, Mr Lazy got up and went to make his breakfast.

We say breakfast, although really it was teatime.

He put the kettle on to make some tea. Kettles take two hours to boil in Sleepyland!

Then he toasted a slice of bread. Bread takes three hours to go brown in Sleepyland.

Toast never gets burnt there!

While he was waiting for his kettle to boil and his bread to toast, Mr Lazy went into the garden of Yawn Cottage – which was where he lived.

He sat down on a chair. And you can probably guess what happened next.

That's right. He yawned, and yawned again, and went to sleep.

Suddenly, he woke up with a jump, which is something that doesn't happen very often to Mr Lazy.

And the reason he woke up with a jump was because of the noise.

"WAKE UP," said the noise.

"WAKEUPWAKEUPWAKEUP."

There were two men standing in front of him.

"I'm Mr Busy," said one of the men.

"And I'm Mr Bustle," said the other.

"Come along now," said Mr Bustle busily.

"We can't have you sleeping all day," added Mr Busy, bustling Mr Lazy to his feet.

"But who are you?" asked Mr Lazy.

"We're Bustle and Busy," they replied.

"Oh," said Mr Lazy.

"Come along now," said Mr Busy, "we haven't got all day."

"But …" said Mr Lazy.

"No time for buts," said Mr Busy. "Or ifs," added Mr Bustle.

"There's the wood to chop and the beds to make and the floors to clean and the coal to get and the windows to polish and the plates to wash and the furniture to dust and the grass to cut and the hedges to clip and the food to cook!"

"And the clothes to mend," added Mr Busy.

"Oh dear," groaned Mr Lazy in a daze. "The wood to clean and the beds to get and the floors to cut and the coal to cook and the windows to make and the plates to mend and the furniture to chop and the grass to wash and the hedges to dust and the clothes to clip?"

He'd got it all completely wrong he was in such a daze.

Then Bustle and Busy set Mr Lazy to work.

Chopping and making and cleaning and getting and polishing and washing and dusting and cutting and clipping and cooking and mending.

Not to mention all the fetching and carrying!

Poor Mr Lazy!

"Now," they said when he'd finished, "it's time for
a walk!

And off they set on the longest walk Mr Lazy had ever
been on.

Mr Lazy is one of those people who never walks when
he has a chance of sitting down, and never sits down
when he has a chance of lying down.

But this day he had no choice. They made him walk for miles and miles and miles, until he felt his legs must be worn right down to his body.

Poor Mr Lazy!

When they arrived back at Yawn Cottage, Mr Busy said, "Right! Now for a run!"

"Oh no," groaned Mr Lazy.

"When I blow this whistle," said Mr Bustle, producing a whistle, "you've got to start running."

"As fast as you can," added Mr Busy.

Mr Lazy groaned a deep groan, and closed his eyes.

Mr Bustle put the whistle to his lips.

"Wheeeeeeeeeeeeee," whistled the whistle.

"Wheeeeeeeeeeeeeeeeeee," went the whistle.

Mr Lazy, poor Mr Lazy, started to run.

But his legs weren't getting him anywhere.

He opened his eyes and looked down to see why.

And the reason his legs weren't getting him anywhere was because he was sitting on a chair in the garden.

And there was no sign of Mr Busy and Mr Bustle!

It had all been a terrible dream!

And the whistle was the whistling kettle boiling in the kitchen!

Mr Lazy heaved a sigh of relief.

And then he went into the kitchen, and sat down to have his breakfast, and to think about his dream.

But you know what happened next, don't you?

"Wake up, Mr Lazy!"

"WAKEUPWAKEUPWAKEUP!"

Fantastic offers for Mr. Men fans!

**Collect all your
Mr. Men or Little Miss books in
these superb durable collector's cases!**

Only £5.99 inc. postage and packaging, these wipe clean, hard wearing cases will give all your Mr. Men and Little Miss books a beautiful new home!

STICK £1 COIN HERE
(For poster only)

**Keep track of your favourite
Mr. Men and Little Miss characters with this brilliant collector's poster, now featuring Mr. Nobody!**

Collect 6 tokens and we will send you a giant-sized double-sided poster! Simply tape a £1 coin in the space provided and fill out the form overleaf.

cut along the dotted line and return this whole page

Only need a few Mr. Men or Little Miss to complete your set? You can order any of the titles on the back of the books from our Mr. Men order line on 0870 787 1724. The majority of orders are delivered in 5 to 7 working days.

TO BE COMPLETED BY AN ADULT

To apply for any of these great offers, ask an adult to complete the details below and send this whole page with the appropriate payment and tokens, to: MR. MEN CLASSIC OFFER PO BOX 715, HORSHAM RH12 5WG

[ ] Please send me a giant-sized double-sided collector's poster.

AND [ ] I enclose 6 tokens and have taped a £1 coin to the other side of this page

[ ] Please send me [ ] Mr. Men Library case(s) and/or [ ] Little Miss Library case(s) at £5.99 each inc P&P

[ ] I enclose a cheque/postal order payable to Egmont UK Limited for £...................

OR [ ] Please debit my MasterCard / Visa / Maestro / Delta account (delete as appropriate) for £...................

Card no. [ ][ ][ ][ ] [ ][ ][ ][ ] [ ][ ][ ][ ] [ ][ ][ ][ ] [ ][ ][ ][ ]   Security code [ ][ ][ ]

Issue no. (if available) [ ]   Start Date [ ][ ] / [ ][ ] / [ ][ ]   Expiry Date [ ][ ] / [ ][ ] / [ ][ ]

Fan's name: ....   Date of birth: ....

Address: ....

....

Postcode: ....

Name of parent / guardian: ....

Email of parent / guardian: ....

Signature of parent / guardian

Offer is only available while stocks last. We reserve the right to change the terms of this offer at any time and we offer a 14 day money back guarantee. Please allow up to 28 days for delivery. This does not affect your statutory rights. Offers apply to UK only.

[ ] We may occasionally wish to send you information about other Egmont books. If you would rather we didn't please tick this box.

cut along the dotted line whole page